THE MASTER

OF THE INN

Robert Herrick

LITERATURE HOUSE / GREGG PRESS
Upper Saddle River, N. J.

9/1972
am. Lit

Republished in 1969 by
LITERATURE HOUSE
an imprint of The Gregg Press
121 Pleasant Avenue
Upper Saddle River, N. J. 07458

Standard Book Number—8398-0779-1
Library of Congress Card—76-96886

Printed in United States of America

ROBERT HERRICK

Robert Herrick was born in Cambridge, Massachusetts, in 1868. His father was a lawyer and a descendant of a New England family that dated back to 1636. Robert attended the Boston Latin School and Harvard, which awarded him a B. A. in 1890. From 1890 to 1893 he was an instructor at the Massachusetts Institute of Technology, which he left to accept a position at the University of Chicago. He became a Professor of English at that institution, and remained there until his retirement in 1923. In 1935 he was appointed secretary to the Governor of the Virgin Islands. He died on the Islands three years later.

Herrick's first stories appeared in the *Harvard Advocate*, and then in the *Harvard Monthly*, which he edited for several years. His first significant work, a novelette entitled *The Man Who Wins*, was published in 1897. This is the story of a scientist whose integrity is undermined by social and financial pressures. The theme of the spiritual agony suffered by the dedicated professional man who finds that his ideals are being destroyed by the morally corrupt forces of commercialism first appears in this story. This theme was to dominate the many works of fiction and non-fiction which followed. He analyzed the business society which he openly loathed, but which, in fact, provided him with subject matter for his art. As he progressed in his art, he showed a widening and deepening of his powers as a satirist, and an increasing concern with the salutary moral influence of women in a rapacious society obsessed with the accumulation of wealth. He perfected the polished, ironical, leisured prose style which is so ideally suited to his subject matter—the careful delineation of a malaise; the rot which has invaded the soul of the American middle class, emanating from the slums it has created. Never have the horrors of "the hunger and sorrow and sordid misery; the grime of living here in Chicago in the sharp discords of the nineteenth century; the brutal rich, the brutalized poor" been described in such flawless prose, and with such careful attention to sociological detail. Herrick rises above the other muckraking novelists in this ability, possessed only by the best literary artists, of making us aware of all of the poisonous implications of man's slavery to business methods, of the ruin of both the body and spirit.

Herrick's secure academic position enabled him to devote the time and energy necessary to the perfection of his art. He was not, like Sinclair Lewis, forced to publish under a deadline, or to resort to sensationalism in order to make his ideas more easily accessible to the reading public. Aware of the abuses of nineteenth-century Capitalism, Herrick was skillful enough to avoid the trap of creating muckraking "novels" like those of Jack London, which were sometimes little more than guidebooks to the slums of various cities, or thinly disguised manifestoes. It was Herrick's relative isolation, and his background; his education in the older, more stable, and gracious society of Boston which enabled him to write so objectively about the ferociously competitive and vulgar city in which he lived and worked. Harvard gave him a set of civilized values, classical and humanistic, with which he could measure and evaluate what he saw in the Midwest. Chicago supplied him with metaphors of human conflict and with a stage upon which his sensitive, socially alienated characters could act out their moral dilemmas. It freed him from the "genteelism" of the East, which probably would have ruined his art.

Herrick refused to become involved in any of the popular reform movements of the day, not out of callousness or indifference, but because of a deep-rooted suspicion that piecemeal legislation was no answer to the problems of industrial America. He retained to the end of his life the conviction that progress occurred when individual men and women chose love, charity, and justice over self-aggrandizement. The cheap, quick, mechanical solutions of the "isms" were self-defeating because they ignored the need for individual reflection and moral decision.

Upper Saddle River, N. J.   F. C. S.
May, 1969

THE MASTER OF THE INN

IN SIMILAR FORM
16mo, Boards, net 50c.

THE
MASTER OF THE INN

BY
Robert Herrick

———

NEW YORK
Charles Scribner's Sons
1918

Published April, **1908**
Second Impression, July, 1908
Third Impression, September, 1908
Fourth Impression, December, 1908
Fifth Impression, December, 1908
Sixth Impression, July, 1909
Seventh Impression, October, 1909
Eighth Impression, January, 1910
Ninth Impression, July, 1910
Tenth Impression, October, 1910
Eleventh Impression, February, 1911
Twelfth Impression, September, 1911
Thirteenth Impression, January, 1912
Fourteenth Impression, August, 1912
Fifteenth Impression, July, 1913
Sixteenth Impression, March, 1914
Seventeenth Impression, January, 1915
Eighteenth Impression, March, 1916
Nineteenth Impression, December, 1916

*The author of "The Master of the Inn"
having received many inquiries as to
what foundation in fact this tale has
wishes to state explicitly that both
incidents and persons are purely im-
aginary, and that so far as he is aware
there is neither Master nor Inn in
existence.*

*Chicago, Ills.,
12 May, 1909.*

THE MASTER OF THE INN

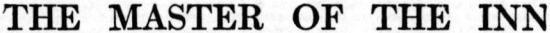

THE
MASTER OF THE INN

I

IT was a plain brick house, three
full stories, with four broad
chimneys, and overhanging
eaves. The tradition was that it
had been a colonial tavern—a dot
among the fir-covered northern hills
on the climbing post-road into Canada. The village scattered along
the road below the inn was called
Albany—and soon forgotten when
the railroad sought an opening
through a valley less rugged, eight
miles to the west.

Rather more than thirty years ago

the Doctor had arrived, one summer day, and opened all the doors and windows of the neglected old house, which he had bought from scattered heirs. He was a quiet man, the Doctor, in middle life then or nearly so; and he sank almost without remark into the world of Albany, where they raise hay and potatoes and still cut good white pine off the hills. Gradually the old brick tavern resumed the functions of life: many buildings were added to it as well as many acres of farm and forest to the Doctor's original purchase of intervale land. The new Master did not open his house to the public, yet he, too, kept a sort of Inn, where men came and stayed a long time. Although no sign now hung from the old elm tree in front of the house,

[4]

nevertheless an ever-widening stream
of humanity mounted the winding
road from White River and passed
through the doors of the Inn, seeking
life. . . .

That first summer the Doctor
brought with him Sam, the Chinaman, whom we all came to know
and love, and also a young man,
who loafed much while the Doctor
worked, and occasionally fished.
This was John Herring—now a
famous architect—and it was from
his designs, sketched those first idle
summer days, that were built all the
additions to the simple old house
—the two low wings in the rear for
the "cells," with the Italian garden
between them; the marble seat curving around the pool that joined the
wings on the west; also the substan-

tial wall that hid the Inn, its terraced gardens and orchards, from
Albanian curiosity. Herring found a
store of red brick in some crumbling
buildings in the neighborhood, and
he discovered the quarry whence
came those thick slabs of purple
slate. The blue-veined marble was
had from a fissure in the hills, and
the Doctor's School made the tiles.

I think Herring never did better
work than in the making over of this
old tavern: he divined that subtle
affinity which exists between north
Italy, with all its art, and our bare
New England; and he dared to graft
boldly one to the other, having the
rear of the Inn altogether Italian
with its portico, its dainty colonnades,
the garden and the fountain and the
pool. From all this one looked down

on the waving grass of the Intervale, which fell away gently to the turbulent White River, then rose again to the wooded hills that folded one upon another, with ever deepening blue, always upward and beyond.

Not all this building at once, to be sure, as the millionaire builds; but a gradual growth over a couple of decades; and all built lovingly by the "Brothers," stone on stone, brick and beam and tile—many a hand taking part in it that came weak to the task and left it sturdy. There was also the terraced arrangement of gardens and orchards on either side of the Inn, reaching to the farm buildings on the one side and to the village on the other. For a time Herring respected the quaint old tavern with its small rooms and pine wain-

[7]

scot; then he made a stately two-
storied hall out of one half where we
dined in bad weather, and a pleasant
study for the Doctor from the rest.
The doors east and west always
stood open in the summer, giving the
rare passer-by a glimpse of that radiant blue heaven among the hills,
with the silver flash of the river in
the middle distance, and a little
square of peaceful garden close at
hand. . . . The tough northern grasses
rustled in the breezes that always
played about Albany; and the scent
of spruce drawn by the hot sun—the
strong resinous breath of the north—
was borne from the woods.

Thus it started, that household of
men in the old Inn at the far end of
Albany village among the northern
hills, with the Doctor and Sam and

Herring, who had been flung aside after his first skirmish with life and was picked up in pure kindness by the Doctor, as a bit of the broken waste of our modern world, and carried off with him out of the city. The young architect returning in due time to the fight—singing—naturally venerated the Doctor as a father; and when a dear friend stumbled and fell in the *via dura* of this life, he whispered to him word of the Inn and its Master—of the life up there among the hills where Man is little and God looks down on his earth. . . . "Oh, you'll understand when you put your eyes on White Face some morning! The Doctor? He heals both body and soul." And this one having heeded spoke the word in turn to others in need—

"to the right sort, who would understand." Thus the custom grew like a faith, and a kind of brotherhood was formed, of those who had found more than health at the Inn—who had found themselves. The Doctor, ever busy about his farms and his woods, his building, and above all his School, soon had on his hands a dozen or more patients or guests, as you might call them, and he set them to work speedily. There was little medicine to be found in the Inn: the sick labored as they could and thus grew strong. . . .

And so, as one was added to another, they began to call themselves in joke "Brothers," and the Doctor, "Father." The older "Brothers" would return to the Inn from all parts of the land, for a few days or a few weeks, to grasp the Doctor's hand, to have a dip in the pool, to try the little brooks among the hills. Young men and middle-aged, and even the old, they came from the cities where the heat of living had scorched them, where they had faltered and doubted the goodness of life. In some way word of the Master had reached them, with this compelling advice—"Go! And tell him I sent you." So from the clinic or the lecture-room, from the office or the mill—wherever men labor with tightening nerves—the needy one started on his long journey. Toward evening he was set down before the plain red face of the Inn. And as the Stranger entered the old hall, a voice was sure to greet him from within somewhere, the deep voice of a hearty man, and presently the Master appeared to welcome the new-comer, resting one hand on his guest's shoulder perhaps, with a yearning affection that ran before knowledge.

"So you've come, my boy," he said. "Herring [or some one] wrote me to look for you."

And after a few more words of greeting, the Doctor beckoned to Sam, and gave the guest over to his hands. Thereupon the Chinaman slippered through tiled passageways to the court, where the Stranger, caught by the beauty and peace so well hidden, lingered a while. The little space within the wings was filled with flowers as far as the yellow water of the pool and the marble bench. In the centre of the court was

an old gray fountain—sent from
Verona by a Brother—from which
the water dropped and ran away
among the flower beds to the pool.
A stately elm tree shaded this place,
flecking the water below. The sun
shot long rays beneath its branches
into the court, and over all there was
an odor of blossoming flowers and
the murmur of bees.

"Bath!" Sam explained, grinning
toward the pool.

With the trickle of the fountain in
his ears the Stranger looked out
across the ripening fields of the Intervale to the noble sky-line of the
Stowe hills. Those little mountains
of the north! Mere hills to all who
know the giants of the earth—not
mountains in the brotherhood of ice
and snow and rock! But in form and

color, in the lesser things that create
the love of men for places, they rise
nobly toward heaven, those little hills!
On a summer day like this their
broad breasts flutter with waving
tree-tops, and at evening depth on
depth of purple mist gathers over
them, dropping into those soft curves
where the little brooks flow, and
mounting even to the sky-line. When
the sun has fallen, there rests a band
of pure saffron, and in the calm and
perfect peace of evening there is a
hint of coming moonlight. Ah, they
are of the fellowship of mountains,
those little hills of Stowe! And when
in winter their flanks are jewelled
with ice and snow, then they raise
their heads proudly to the stars, calling across the frozen valleys to their
greater brethren in the midriff of

the continent—"Behold, we also are
hills, in the sight of the Lord!" . . .
Meantime Sam, with Oriental ease,
goes slipping along the arcade until
he comes to a certain oak door,
where he drops your bag, and dis-
appears, having saluted. It is an
ample and lofty room, and on the
outer side of it hangs a little balcony
above the orchard, from which there
is a view of the valley and the woods
beyond, and from somewhere in the
fields the note of the thrush rises.
The room itself is cool, of a gray
tone, with a broad fireplace, a heavy
table, and many books. Otherwise
there are bed and chairs and dress-
ing-table, the necessities of life aus-
terely provided. And Peace! God,
what Peace to him who has escaped
from the furnace men make! It is as

if he had come all the way to the end
of the world, and found there a great
still room of peace.

Soon a bell sounds—with a strange
vibration as though in distant lands
it had summoned many a body of
men together—and the household as-
sembles under the arcade. If it is
fair and not cold, Sam and his helpers
bring out the long narrow table and
place it, as Veronese places his feast-
ers, lengthwise beneath the colon-
nade, and thus the evening meal is
served. A fresh, coarse napkin is laid
on the bare board before each man,
no more than enough for all those
present, and the Doctor sits in the
middle, serving all. There are few
dishes, and for the most part such
as may be got at home there in the
hills. There is a pitcher of cider at

one end and a pitcher of mild white
wine at the other, and the men eat
and drink, with jokes and talk—the
laughter of the day. (The novice
might feel only the harmony of it
all, but later he will learn how many
considered elements go to the making of Peace.) Afterward, when Sam
has brought pipes and tobacco, the
Master leads the way to the sweeping
semicircle of marble seat around the
pool with the leafy tree overhead; and
there they sit into the soft night, talking of all things, with the glow of
pipes, until one after another slips
away to sleep. For as the Master
said, "Talk among men in common
softens the muscles of the mind and
quickens the heart." Yet he loved
most to hear the talk of others.

Thus insensibly for the Novice there

begins the life of the place, opening
in a gentle and persistent routine that
takes him in its flow and carries
him on with it. He finds Tradition
and Habit all about him, in the
ordered, unconscious life of the Inn,
to which he yields without question.
. . . Shortly after dawn the bell
sounds, and then the men meet at
the pool, where the Doctor is always first. A plunge into the yellow
water which is flecked with the
fallen leaves, and afterward to each
man's room there is brought a
large bowl of coffee and hot milk,
with bread and eggs and fruit. What
more he craves may be found in
the hall.

Soon there is a tap on the new-
comer's door, and a neighborly voice
calls out—"We all go into the fields

every morning, you know. You must
earn your dinner, the Doctor says, or
borrow it!" So the Novice goes forth
to earn his first dinner with his hands.
Beyond the gardens and the orchards
are the barns and sheds, and a
vista of level acres of hay and potatoes and rye, the bearing acres of the
farm, and beyond these the woods
on the hills. "Nearly a thousand
acres, fields and woods," the neigh-
bor explains. "Oh, there's plenty to
do all times!" Meantime the Doctor
strides ahead through the wet grass,
his eyes roaming here and there, in-
quiring the state of his land. And
watching him the newcomer be-
lieves that there is always much to
be done wherever the Doctor leads.

It may be July and hay time—all
the intervale grass land is mowed by

hand—there is a sweat-breaking task!
Or it may be potatoes to hoe. Or
later in the season the apples have to
be gathered—a pleasant pungent job,
filling the baskets and pouring them
into the fat-bellied barrels. But whatever the work may be the Doctor
keeps the Novice in his mind, and
as the sun climbs high over the Stowe
hills, he taps the new one on the
shoulder—"Better stop here to-day,
my boy! You'll find a good tree
over there by the brook for a
nap. . . ."

Under that particular tree in the
tall timothy, there is the coolest spot,
and the Novice drowses, thinking of
those wonderful mowers in *Anna*, as
he gazes at the marching files eating
their way through the meadow until
his eyelids fall and he sleeps, the rip-

ple of waving timothy in his ears. At noon the bell sounds again from the Inn, and the men come striding homeward wiping the sweat from their faces. They gather at the swimming pool, and still panting from their labor strip off their wet garments, then plunge one after another, like happy boys. From bath to room, and a few minutes for fresh clothes, and all troop into the hall, which is dark and cool. The old brick walls of the tavern never held a gayer lot of guests.

From this time on each one is his own master; there is no common toil. The farmer and his men take up the care of the farm, and the Master usually goes down to his School, in company with some of the Brothers. Each one finds his own way

of spending the hours till sunset—
some fishing or shooting, according
to the season; others, in tennis o
games with the boys of the School;
and some reading or loafing—until
the shadows begin to fall across the
pool into the court, and Sam brings
out the long table for dinner.

The seasons shading imperceptibly
into one another vary the course of
the day. Early in September the men
begin to sit long about the hall-fire
of an evening, and when the snow
packs hard on the hills there is wood-
cutting to be done, and in early
spring it is the carpenter's shop. So
the form alters, but the substance
remains—work and play and rest. . . .

To each one a time will come when
the Doctor speaks to him alone. At
some hour, before many days have

passed, the Novice will find himself
with those large eyes resting on his
face, searchingly. It may be in the
study after the others have scattered,
or at the pool where the Master loved
to sit beneath the great tree and hear
his "confessions," as the men called
these talks. At such times, when the
man came to remember it afterward,
the Doctor asked few questions, said
little, but listened. He had the con-
fessing ear! And as if by chance his
hand would rest on the man's arm or
shoulder. For he said—"Touch
speaks: soul flows through flesh into
soul."

Thus he sat and confessed his patients one after another, and his dark
eyes seemed familiar with all man's
woes, as if he had listened always.
Men said to him what they had never

before let pass their lips to man or woman, what they themselves scarce looked at in the gloom of their souls. Unawares it slipped from them, the reason within the reason for their ill, the ultimate cause of sorrow. From the moment they had revealed to him this hidden thing—had slipped the leash on their tongues—it seemed no longer to be feared. "Trouble evaporates, being properly aired," said the Doctor. And already in the troubled one's mind the sense of the confused snarl of life began to lessen and veils began to descend between him and it. . . . "For you must learn to forget," counselled the Doctor, "forget day by day until the recording soul beneath your mind is clean. Therefore —work, forget, be new!" . . .

A self-important young man, much

concerned with himself, once asked the Master:

"Doctor, what is the regimen that you would recommend to me?"

And we all heard him say in reply—

"The potatoes need hilling, and then you'll feel like having a dip in the pool."

The young man, it seems, wrote back to the friend in the city who had sent him—"This Doctor cannot understand my case: he tells me to dig potatoes and bathe in a swimming pool. That is all! All!" But the friend, who was an old member of the Brotherhood, telegraphed back— "Dig and swim, you fool!" Sam took the message at the telephone while we were dining, and repeated it faithfully to the young man within the hearing of all. A laugh rose that was hard in dying, and I think the Doctor's lips wreathed in smile. . . . In the old days they say the Master gave medicine like other doctors. That was when he spent part of the year in the city and had an office there and believed in drugs. But as he gave up going to the city, the stock of drugs in the cabinet at the end of the study became exhausted, and was never renewed. All who needed medicine were sent to an old Brother, who had settled down the valley at Stowe. "He knows more about pills than I do," the Doctor said. "At least he can give you the stuff with confidence." Few of the inmates of the Inn ever went to Stowe, though Dr. Williams was an excellent physician. And it was from about this time that we began to drop the title of doctor, calling him instead the Master; and the younger men sometimes, Father. He seemed to like these new terms, as denoting affection and respect for his authority.

By the time that we called him Master, the Inn had come to its maturity. Altogether it could hold eighteen guests, and if more came, as in midsummer or autumn, they lived in tents in the orchard or in the hill camps. The Master was still adding to the forest land—fish and game preserve the village people called it; for the Master was a hunter and a fisherman. But up among those curving hills, when he looked out through the waving trees, measuring by eye a fir or a pine, he would say, nodding his head—"Boys, behold my

heirs—from generation to generation!"

He was now fifty and had ceased
altogether to go to the city. There
were ripe men in the great hospitals
that still remembered him as a young
man in the medical school; but he
had dropped out, they said—why?
He might have answered that, instead of following the beaten path,
he had spoken his word to the world
through men—and spoken widely.
For there was no break in the stream
of life that flowed upward to the
old Inn. The "cells" were always
full, winter and summer. Now there
were coming children of the older
Brothers, and these, having learned
the ways of the place from their
fathers, were already house-broken,
as we said, when they came. They

knew that no door was locked about the Inn, but that if they returned after ten it behooved them to come in by the pool and make no noise. They knew that when the first ice formed on the pool, then they were not expected to get out of bed for the morning plunge. They knew that there was an old custom which no one ever forgot, and that was to put money in the house-box behind the hall door on leaving, at least something for each day of the time spent, and as much more as one cared to give. For, as every one knew, all in the box beyond the daily expense went to maintain the School on the road below the village. So the books of the Inn were easy to keep—there was never a word about money in the place—but I know that many a

large sum of money was found in
this box, and the School never wanted
means.

That I might tell more of what took
place in the Inn, and what the Master
said, and the sort of men one found
there, and the talk we all had summer evenings beside the pool and winter nights in the hall! Winter, I think,
was the best time of all the year,
the greatest beauty and the greatest joy, from the first fall of the
snow to the yellow brook water and
the floating ice in White River. Then
the broad velvety shadows lay on the
hills between the stiff spruces, then
came rosy mornings out of darkness
when you knew that some good thing
was waiting for you in the world.
After you had drunk your bowl of
coffee, you got your axe and followed

the procession of choppers, who were carefully foresting the Doctor's woods. In the spring, when the little brooks had begun to run down the slopes, there was road making and mending; for the Master kept in repair most of the roads about Albany, grinding the rock in his pit, saying that—"a good road is one sure blessing."

And the dusks I shall never forget —those gold and violet moments with the light of immortal heavens behind the rampart of hills; and the nights, so still, so still like everlasting death, each star set jewel-wise in a black sky above a white earth. How splendid it was to turn out of the warm hall where we had been reading and talking into the frosty court, with the thermometer at twenty below and still falling, and look down across the broad white valley, marked by the streak of bushy alders where the dumb river flowed, up to the little frozen water courses among the hills, up above where the stars glittered! You took your way to your room in the silence, rejoicing that it was all so, that somewhere in this tumultuous world of ours there was hidden all this beauty and the secret of living; and that you were of the brotherhood of those who had found it. . . .

Thus was the Inn and its Master in the year when he touched sixty, and his hair and beard were more white than gray.

II

THEN there came to the Inn one day in the early part of the summer a new guest—a man about fifty, with an aging, worldly face. Bill, the Albany stage man, had brought him from Island Junction, and on the way had answered all his questions, discreetly, reckoning in his wisdom that his passenger was "one of those queer folks that went up to the old Doctor's place." For there was something smart and fashionable about the stranger's appearance that made Bill uncomfortable.

"There," he said, as he pulled up outside the red brick house and pointed over the wall into the garden, "mos' likely you'll find the old man fussin' 'round somewheres inside there, if he hain't down to the School," and he drove off with the people's mail.

The stranger looked back through the village street, which was as silent as a village street should be at four o'clock on a summer day. Then he muttered to himself, whimsically, "Mos' likely you'll find the old man fussin' 'round somewheres inside!" Well, *what next?* And he glanced at the homely red brick building with the cold eye of one who has made many goings out and comings in, and to whom novelty offers little entertainment. As he stood there (thinking possibly of that early train from the junction on the morrow) the hall door opened wide, and an

[34]

oldish man with white eye-brows and black eyes appeared. He was dressed in a linen suit that deepened the dark tan of his face and hands. He said:

"You are Dr. Augustus Norton?"

"And you," the Stranger replied with a graceful smile, "are the Master—and this is the Inn!"

He had forgotten what Percival called the old boy—forgot everything these days—had tried to remember the name all the way up—nevertheless, he had turned it off well! So the two looked at each other—one a little younger as years go, but with lined face and shaking fingers; the other solid and self-contained, with less of that ready language which comes from always jostling with nimble wits. But as they stood there, each saw a Man and an Equal.

"The great surgeon of St. Jerome's," said our Master in further welcome.

"Honored by praise from your lips!" Thus the man of the city lightly turned the compliment, and extended his hand, which the Master took slowly, gazing meanwhile steadily at his guest.

"Pray come into my house," said the Master of the Inn, with more stateliness of manner than he usually had with a new Brother. But, it may be said, Dr. Augustus Norton had the most distinguished name of that day in his profession. He followed the Master to his study, with uncertain steps, and sinking into a deep chair before the smouldering ashes looked at his host with a sad grin— "Perhaps you'll give me something— the journey, you know? . . ."

Two years before the head surgeon
of St. Jerome's had come to the
hospital of a morning to perform
some operation—one of those affairs
for which he was known from coast
to coast. As he entered the officers'
room that day, with the arrogant
eye of the commander-in-chief, one
of his aides looked at him sus-
piciously, then glanced again—and
the great surgeon felt those eyes upon
him when he turned his back. And he
knew why! Something was wrong
with him. Nevertheless in glum silence he made ready to operate. But
when the moment came, and he was
about to take the part of God toward
the piece of flesh lying in the ether
sleep before him, he hesitated. Then,
in the terrible recoil of Fear, he
turned back.

[37]

"Macroe!" he cried to his assistant, "you will have to operate. I cannot— I am not well!"

There was almost panic, but Macroe was a man, too, and proceeded to do his work without a word. The great surgeon, his hands now trembling beyond disguise, went back to the officers' room, took off his white robes, and returned to his home. There he wrote his resignation to the directors of St. Jerome's, and his resignation from other offices of honor and responsibility. Then he sent for a medical man, an old friend, and held out his shaking hand to him:

"The damn thing won't go," he said, pointing also to his head.

"Too much work," the doctor replied, of course.

But the great surgeon, who was a man of clear views, added impersonally, "Too much everything, I guess!"

There followed the usual prescription, making the sick man a wanderer and pariah—first to Europe, "to get rid of me," the surgeon growled; then to Georgia for golf, to Montana for elk, to Canada for salmon, and so forth. Each time the sick man returned with a thin coat of tan that peeled off in a few days, and with those shaking hands that suggested immediately another journey to another climate. Until it happened finally that the men of St. Jerome's who had first talked of the date of their chief's return merely raised their eyebrows at the mention of his name.

"Done for, poor old boy!" and the

great surgeon read it with his lynx
eyes, in the faces of the men he met
at his clubs. His mouth drew together sourly and his back sloped.
"Fifty-two," he muttered. "God,
that is too early—something ought to
pull me together." So he went on
trying this and that, while his friends
said he was "resting," until he had
slipped from men's thoughts.

One day Percival of St. Jerome's,
one of those boys he had growled at
and cursed in former times, met him
crawling down the avenue to his
quietest club, and the old surgeon
took him by the arm—he was gray
in face and his neck was wasting
away—and told the story of his
troubles—as he would to anyone
these days. The young man listened
respectfully. Then he spoke of the old

Inn, of the Brotherhood, of the Master and what he had done for miserable men, who had despaired. The famous surgeon, shaking his head as one who has heard of these miracles many times and found them naught, was drinking it all in, nevertheless.

"He takes a man," said the young surgeon, "who doesn't want to live and makes him fall in love with life."

Dr. Augustus Norton sniffed.

"In love with life! That's good! If your Wonder of the Ages can make a man of fifty fall in love with anything, I must try him." He laughed a sneering laugh, the feeble merriment of doubt.

"Ah, Doctor!" cried the young man, "you must go and live with the Master. And then come back to us at St. Jerome's: for we need you!"

And the great surgeon, touched to the heart by these last words, said:

"Well, what's the name of your miracle-worker, and where is he to be found? . . . I might as well try all the cures—write a book on 'em one of these days!" . . .

So he came by the stage to the gate of the old Inn, and the Master, who had been warned by a telegram from the young doctor only that morning, stood at his door to welcome his celebrated guest.

He put him in the room of state above the study, a great square room at the southwest, overlooking the wings and the flower-scented garden, the pool, and the waving grass fields beyond, dotted with tall elms—all freshly green.

"Not a bad sort of place," murmured the weary man, "and there must be trout in those brooks up yonder. Well, it will do for a week or two, if there's fishing." . . . Then the bell sounded for dinner which was served for the first time that season out of doors in the soft twilight. The Brothers had gathered in the court beside the fountain, young men and middle-aged—all having bent under some burden, which they were now learning to carry easily. They stood about the hall door until the distinguished Stranger appeared, and he walked between them to the place of honor at the Master's side. Every one at the long table was named to the great surgeon, and then with the coming of the soup he was promptly forgotten, while the talk of the day's work and the morrow's rose vigorously from all sides. It was a question of the old mill, which had given way. An engineer among the company described what would have to be done to get at the foundations. And a young man who happened to sit next to the surgeon explained that the Master had re-opened an old mill above the Inn in the Intervale, where he ground corn and wheat and rye with the old water-wheel; for the country people, who had always got their grain ground there, complained when the mill had been closed. It seemed to the Stranger that the dark coarse bread which was served was extraordinarily good, and he wondered if the ancient process had anything to do with it and he resolved to see the old mill. Then the young man said

something about bass: there was a
cool lake up the valley, which had
been stocked. The surgeon's eye
gleamed. Did he know how to fish
for bass! Why, before this boy—yes,
he would go at five in the morning,
sharp. . . . After the meal, while the
blue wreaths of smoke floated across
the flowers and the talk rose and
fell in the court, the Master and his
new guest were seated alone beneath
the great elm. The surgeon could
trace the Master's face in the still
waters of the pool at their feet, and
it seemed to him like a finely cut
cameo, with gentle lines about the
mouth and eyes that relieved the
thick nose. Nevertheless he knew by
certain instinct that they were not of
the same kind. The Master was very
silent this night, and his guest felt

[45]

that some mystery, some vacuum existed between them, as he gazed on the face in the water. It was as if the old man were holding him off at arm's length while he looked into him. But the great surgeon, who was used to the amenities of city life, resolved to make his host talk:

"Extraordinary sort of place you have here! I don't know that I have ever seen anything just like it. And what is your System?"

"What is my System?" repeated the Master wonderingly.

"Yes! Your method of building these fellows up—electricity, diet, massage, baths—what is your line?" An urbane smile removed the offence of the banter.

"I have no System!" the Master replied thoughtfully. "I live my life

[46]

here with my work, and those you see
come and live with me as my friends."

"Ah, but you have ideas . . . extraordinary success . . . so many cases,"
the great man muttered, confused
by the Master's steady gaze.

"You will learn more about us
after you have been here a little time.
You will see, and the others will help
you to understand. To-morrow we
work at the mill, and the next day
we shall be in the gardens—but you
may be too tired to join us. And we
bathe here, morning and noon. Harvey will tell you all our customs."

The celebrated surgeon of St. Jerome's wrote that night to an old
friend: "And the learned doctor's
prescription seems to be to dig in
the garden and bathe in a great
pool! A daffy sort of place—but I

[47]

am going bass fishing to-morrow at five with a young man, who is just the right age for a son! So to bed, but I suspect that I shall see you soon—novelties wear out quickly at my years."

Just here there entered that lovely night wind, rising far away beyond the low lakes to the south—it soughed through the room, swaying the draperies, sighing, sighing, and it blew out the candle. The sick man looked down on the court below, white in the moonlight, and his eyes roved farther to the dark orchard, and the great barns and the huddled cattle.

"Quite a bit of country here!" the surgeon murmured. As he stood there looking into the misty light which covered the Intervale, up to the great hills above which floated luminous cloud banks, the chorus of an old song rose from below where the pipes gleamed in the dark about the pool. He leaned out into the air, filled with all the wild scent of green fields, and added under a sort of compulsion—"And a good place, enough!"

He went to bed to a deep sleep, and over his tired, worldly face the night wind passed gently, stripping leaf by leaf from his weary mind that heavy coating of care which he had wrapped about him in the course of many years.

Dr. Augustus Norton did not return at the end of one week, nor of two. The city saw him, indeed, no more that year. It was said that a frisky, rosy ghost of the great surgeon had slipped into St. Jerome's near Christmas—had skipped through a club or two and shaken hands about pretty generally—and disappeared. Sometimes letters came from him with an out-of-the-way postmark on them, saying in a jesting tone that he was studying the methods of an extraordinary country doctor, who seemed to cure men by touch. "He lives up here among the hills in forty degrees of frost, and if I am not mistaken he is nearer the Secret than all of you pill slingers"— (for he was writing a mere doctor of medicine!). "Anyhow I shall stay on until I learn the Secret—or my host turns me out; for life up here seems as good to me as ice-cream and kisses to a girl of sixteen. . . . Why should I go back mucking about with you fellows—just yet? I caught a five-pounder yesterday, and *ate* him!"

There are many stories of the great surgeon that have come to me from those days. He was much liked, especially by the younger men, after the first gloom had worn off, and he began to feel the blood run once more. He had a joking way with him that made him a good table companion, and the Brothers pretending that he would become the historian of the order taught him all the traditions of the place. "But the Secret, the Secret! Where is it?" he would demand jestingly. One night—it was at table and all were there—Harvey asked him:

"Has the Master confessed you?"

"'Confessed me'?" repeated the surgeon. "What's that?"

A sudden silence fell on all, because this was the one thing never spoken of, at least in public. Then the Master, who had been silent all that evening, turned the talk to other matters.

The Master, to be sure, gave this distinguished guest all liberties, and they often talked together as men of the same profession. And the surgeon witnessed all—the mending of the mill, the planting and the hoeing and the harvesting, the preparations for the long winter, the chopping and the road-making—all, and he tested it with his hands. "Not bad sport," he would say, "with so many sick-well young men about to help!"

But meanwhile the "secret" escaped the keen mind, though he sought for it daily.

"You give no drugs, Doctor," he

complained. "You're a scab on the profession!"

"The drugs gave out," the Master explained, "and I neglected to order more. . . . There's always Bert Williams at Stowe, who can give you anything you might want—shall I send for him, Doctor?"

There was laughter all about, and when it died down the great surgeon returned to the attack.

"Well, come, tell us now what you do believe in? Magic, the laying on of hands? Come, there are four doctors here, and we have the right to know—or we'll report you!"

"I believe," said the Master solemnly, in reply to the banter, "I believe in Man and in God." And there followed such talk as had never been in the old hall; for the

surgeon was, after his kind, a ma-
terialist and pushed the Master for
definition. The Master believed, as I
recall it, that Disease could not be
cured, for the most part. No chem-
istry would ever solve the mystery of
pain! But Disease could be ignored,
and the best way to forget pain was
through labor. Not labor merely for
oneself; but also something for others.
Wherefore the School, around which
the Inn and the farm and all had
grown. For he told us then that he
had bought the Inn as a home for
his boys, the waste product of the
city. Finding the old tavern too
small for his purpose and seeing how
he should need helpers, he had en-
couraged ailing men to come to live
with him and to cure themselves by
curing others. Without that School

below in the valley, with its work-shops and cottages, there would have been no Inn!

As for God—that night he would go no further, and the surgeon said rather flippantly, we all thought, that the Master had left little room in his world for God, anyhow—he had made man so large. It was a stormy August evening, I remember, when we had been forced to dine within on account of the gusty rain that had come after a still, hot day. The valley seemed filled with murk, which was momentarily torn by fire, revealing the trembling leaves upon the trees. When we passed through the arcade to reach our rooms, the surgeon pointed out into this sea of fire and darkness, and muttered with a touch of irony—

"HE seems to be talking for him self this evening!"

Just then a bolt shot downward, revealing with large exaggeration the hills, the folded valleys—the descents.

"It's like standing on a thin plank in a turbulent sea!" the surgeon remarked wryly. "Ah, my boy, Life's like that!" and he disappeared into his room.

Nevertheless, it was that night he wrote to his friend: "I am getting nearer this Mystery, which I take to be, the inner heart of it, a mixture of the Holy Ghost and Sweat—with a good bath afterward! But the old boy is the mixer of the Pills, mind you, and he *is* a Master! Most likely I shall never get hold of the heart of it: for somehow, yet with all courtesy,

he keeps me at a distance. I have
never been 'confessed,' whatever that
may be—an experience that comes to
the youngest boy among them! Perhaps the Doctor thinks that old fellows like you and me have only dead
sins to confess, which would crumble
to dust if exposed. But there is a
sting in very old sins, I think—for
instance—oh! if you were here to-
night, I should be as foolish as a
woman. . . ."

The storm that night struck one of
the school buildings and killed a lad.
In the morning the Master and the
surgeon set out for the School Village,
which was lower in the valley beyond
Albany. It was warm and clear at
the Inn; but thick mist wreaths still
lay heavily over the Intervale. The
hills all about glittered as in October.

and there was in the air that laughing peace, that breath of sweet plenty which comes the morning after a storm. The two men followed the foot-path, which wound downward from the Inn across the Intervale. The sun filled the windless air, sucking up the spicy odors of the tangled path—fern and balsam and the mother scent of earth and rain and sun. The new green rioted over the dead leaves. . . . The Master closely observing his guest, remarked:

"You seem quite well, Doctor. I suppose you will be leaving us soon?"

"Leaving?" the surgeon questioned slowly, as if a secret dread had risen at the Master's hint of departure. "Yes," he admitted, after a time, "I suppose I am what you would call well—well enough. But something

still clogs within me. It may be the memory of Fear. I am afraid of myself!"

"Afraid? You need some test, perhaps. That will come sooner or later; we need not hurry it!"

"No, we need not hurry!"

Yet he knew well enough that the Inn never sheltered drones, and that many special indulgences had been granted him: he had borrowed freely from the younger Brothers—of their time and strength. He thought complacently of the large cheque which he should drop into the house-box on his departure. With it the Master would be able to build a new cottage or a small hospital for the School.

"Some of them," mused the Master, "never go back to the machine that

once broke them. They stay about here and help me—buy a farm and revert! But for the most part they are keen to get back to the fight, as is right and best. Sometimes when they loiter too long, I shove them out of the nest!"

"And I am near the shoving point?" his companion retorted quickly. "So I must leave all your dear boys and Peace and Fishing and *you!* Suppose so, suppose so! . . . Doctor, you've saved my life—oh, hang it, that doesn't tell the story. But even *I* can feel what it is to live at the Inn!"

Instinctively he grasped his host by the arm—he was an impulsive man. But the Master's arm did not respond to the clasp; indeed, a slight shiver seemed to shake it, so that the

surgeon's hand fell away while the
Master said:

"I am glad to have been of service
—to you—yes, especially to *you*. . . ."

They came into the school village,
a tiny place of old white houses,
very clean and trim, with a number
of sweeping elms along the narrow
road. A mountain brook turned an
old water-wheel, supplying power
for the workshops where the boys
were trained. The great surgeon had
visited the place many times in company with the Master, and though
he admired the order and economy
of the institution, and respected its
purpose—that is, to create men out
of the refuse of society—to tell the
truth, the place bored him a trifle.
This morning they went directly to
the little cottage that served as in-

firmary, where the dead boy had
been brought. He was a black-haired
Italian, and his lips curved upward
pleasantly. The Master putting his
hand on the dead boy's brow as he
might have done in life stood looking
at the face.

"I've got a case in the next room,
I'd like to have your opinion on,
Doctor," the young physician said
in a low tone to the surgeon, and the
two crossed the passage into the
neighboring room. The surgeon fast-
ened his eyes on the sick lad's body:
here was a case he understood, a
problem with a solution. The old
Master coming in from the dead
stood behind the two.

"Williams," the surgeon said, "it's
so, sure enough—you must operate—
at once!"

"I was afraid it was that," the younger man replied. "But how can I operate here?"

The surgeon shrugged his shoulders — "He would never reach the city!"

"Then I must, you think——"

The shrewd surgeon recognized Fear in the young man's voice. Quick the thrill shot through his nerves, and he cried, "I will operate, *now*."

In half an hour it was over, and the Master and the surgeon were leaving the village, climbing up by the steep path under the blazing noon sun. The Master glanced at the man by his side, who strode along confidently, a trifle of a swagger in his buoyant steps. The Master remarked:

"The test came, and you took it— splendidly."

"Yes," the great surgeon replied,

smiling happily, "it's all there, Doctor, the old power. I believe I am about ready to get into harness again!" After they had walked more of the way without speaking, the surgeon added, as to himself—"But there are other things to be feared!"

Though the Master looked at him closely he invited no explanation, and they finished their homeward walk without remark.

It soon got about among the inmates of the Inn what a wonderful operation the surgeon of St. Jerome's had performed, and it was rumored that at the beginning of autumn he would go back to his old position. Meantime the great surgeon enjoyed the homage that men always pay to power, the consideration of his fel-

lows. He had been much liked; but
now that the Brothers knew how
soon he was to leave them, they surrounded him with those attentions
that men most love, elevating him
almost to the rank of the Master—
and they feared him less. His fame
spread, so that from some mill beyond Stowe they brought to the Inn
a desperate case, and the surgeon
operated again successfully, demon-
strating that he was once more master of his art, and master of himself.
So he stayed on merely to enjoy his
triumph and escape the dull season
in the city.

It was a wonderful summer, that!
The fitful temper of the north played
in all its moods. There were days
when the sun shone tropically down
into the valleys, without a breath of

air, when the earthy, woodsy smells were strong—and the nights—perfect stillness and peace, as if some spirit of the air were listening for love words on the earth. The great elms along Albany road hung their branches motionless, and when the moon came over behind the house the great hills began to swim ghostly, vague—beyond, always beyond! . . . And then there were the fierce storms that swept up the valley and hung growling along the hills for days, and afterward, sky-washed and clear, the westerly breeze would come tearing down the Intervale, drying the earth before it. . . . But each day there was a change in the sound and the smell of the fields and the woods— in the quick race of the northern summer—a change that the surgeon,

[66]

fishing up the tiny streams, felt and
noted. Each day, so radiant with its
abundant life, sounded some under-
note of fulfilment and change—
speaking beforehand of death to
come.

Toward the end of August a snap
of cold drove us in-doors for the night
meal. Then around the fire there was
great talk between the Master and
the surgeon, a sort of battle of the
soul, to which we others paid silent
attention. For wherever those nights
the talk might rise, in the little rills
of accidental words, it always flowed
down to the deep underlying thoughts
of men. And in those depths, as I
said, these two wrestled with each
other. The Master, who had grown
silent of late years, woke once more
with fire. The light, keen thrusts of

the surgeon, who argued like a fencer, roused his whole being; and as day by day it went on we who watched saw that in a way the talk of these two men set forth the great conflict of conflicts, that deepest fissure of life and belief anent the Soul and the Body. And the Master, who had lived his faiths by his life before our eyes, was being worsted in the argument! The great surgeon had the better mind, and he had seen all of life that one may see with eyes. . . .

They were talking of the day of departure for the distinguished guest, and arranging for some kind of triumphal procession to escort him to White River. But he would not set the time, shrinking from this act, as if all were not yet done. There came

a warm, glowing day early in September, and at night after the pipes
were lighted the surgeon and the
Master strolled off in the direction
of the pool, arm in arm. There had
been no talk that day, the surgeon
apparently shrinking from coming to
the last grapple with one whose
faiths were so important to him as
the Master's.

"The flowers are dying: they tell
me it's time to move on," said the
surgeon. "And yet, my dear host, I
go without the Secret, without under-
standing All!"

"Perhaps there is no inner Secret,"
the Master smiled. "It is all here
before you."

"I know that—you have been very
good to me, shared everything. If I
have not learned the Secret, it is my

fault, my incapacity. But—" and the
gay tone dropped quickly and a
flash of bitterness succeeded— "I at
least know that there *is* a Secret!"

They sat down on the marble bench
and looked into the water, each thinking his thoughts. Suddenly the surgeon began to speak, hesitantly, as if
there had long been something in his
mind that he was compelled to say.

"My friend," he said, "I too have
something to tell—the cause within
the cause, the reason of the reason—
at least, sometimes I think it is! The
root reason for all—unhappiness, de-
feat, for the shaking hand and the
jesting voice. And I want you to hear
it—if you will."

The Master raised his face from the
pool but said never a word. The surgeon continued, his voice trembling

at times, though he spoke slowly, evidently trying to banish all feeling.

"It is a common enough story at the start, at least among men of our kind. You know that I was trained largely in Europe. My father had the means to give me the best, and time to take it in. So I was over there, before I came back to St. Jerome's, three, four years at Paris, Munich, Vienna, all about. . . . While I was away I lived as the others, for the most part —you know our profession—and youth. The rascals are pretty much the same to-day, I judge from what my friends say of their sons! Well, at least I worked like the devil, and was decent. . . . Oh, it isn't for that I'm telling the tale! I was ambitious, then. And the time came to go back, as it does in the end, and I took a few weeks' run through Italy as a final taste of the lovely European thing, and came down to Naples to get the boat for New York. I've never been back to Naples since, and that was twenty-six years ago this autumn. But I can see the city always as it was then! The seething human hive—the fellows piling in the freight to the music of their songs—the fiery mouth of Vesuvius up above. And the soft, dark night with just a plash of waves on the quay!''

The Master listened, his eyes again buried in the water at their feet.

''Well, *she* was there on board, of course—looking out also into that warm dark night and sighing for all that was to be lost so soon. There were few passengers in those days.

. . . She was my countrywoman, and beautiful, and there was something— at least so I thought then—of especial sweetness in her eyes, something strong in her heart. She was engaged to a man living somewhere in the States, and she was going back to marry him. Why she was over there then I forget, and it is of no importance. I think that the man was a doctor, too—in some small city. . . . I loved her!"

The Master raised his eyes from the pool and leaning on his folded arms looked into the surgeon's face.

"I am afraid I never thought much about that other fellow—never have to this day! That was part of the brute I am—to see only what is before my eyes. And I knew by the time we had swung into the Atlantic that

I wanted that woman as I had never
wanted things before. She stirred me,
mind and all. Of course it might have
been some one else—any one you
will say—and if she had been an
ordinary young girl, it might have
gone differently? It is one of the
things we can't tell in this life. There
was something in that woman that
was big all through and roused the
spirit in me. I never knew man or
woman who thirsted more for great-
ness, for accomplishment. Perhaps
the man she was to marry gave her
little to hope for—probably it was
some raw boy-and-girl affair such as
we have in America. . . . The days
went by, and it was clearer to both
of us what must be. But we didn't
speak of it. She found in me, I suppose, the power, the sort of thing she

had missed in the other. I was to do
all those grand things she was so hot
after. I have done some of them too.
But that was when she had gone
and I no longer needed her. . . . I
needed her then, and I took her—
that is all.

"The detail is old and dim—and
what do you care to hear of a young
man's loves! Before we reached port
it was understood between us. I told
her I wanted her to leave the other
chap—he was never altogether clear
to me—and to marry me as soon as
she could. We did not stumble or
slide into it, not in the least: we
looked it through and through—that
was her kind and mine. How she
loved to look life in the face! I have
found few women who like that.
. . . In the end she asked me not to

come near her the last day. She would write me the day after we had landed, either yes or no. So she kissed me, and we parted still out at sea."

All the Brothers had left the court and the arcades, where they had been strolling, and old Sam was putting out the Inn lights. But the two men beside the pool made no movement. The west wind still drew in down the valley with summer warmth and ruffled the water at their feet.

"My father met me at the dock— you know he was the first surgeon at St. Jerome's before me. My mother was with him. . . . But as she kissed me I was thinking of that letter. . . . I knew it would come. Some things must! Well, it came."

The silent listener bent his head,

and the surgeon mused on his passionate memory. At last the Master whispered in a low voice that hardly reached into the night:

"Did you make her happy?"

The surgeon did not answer the question at once.

"Did you make her happy?" the old man demanded again, and his voice trembled this time with such intensity that his companion looked at him wonderingly. And in those dark eyes of the Master's he read something that made him shrink away. Then for the third time the old man demanded sternly:

"Tell me—did you make her happy?"

It was the voice of one who had a right to know, and the surgeon whispered back slowly:

"Happy? No, my God! Perhaps
at first, in the struggle, a little. But
afterward there was too much—too
many things. It went, the inspira-
tion and the love. I broke her heart
—she left me! That—that is *my*
Reason!"

"It *is* the Reason! For you took all,
all—you let her give all, and you
gave her—what?"

"Nothing—she died."

"I know—she died."

The Master had risen, and with
folded arms faced his guest, a pitying
look in his eyes. The surgeon covered
his face with his hands, and after a
long time said:

"So you knew this?"

"Yes, I knew!"

"And knowing you let me come
here. You took me into your house,

[78]

you healed me, you gave me back my life!"

And the Master replied with a firm voice:

"I knew, and I gave you back your life." In a little while he explained more softly: "You and I are no longer young men who feel hotly and settle such a matter with hate. We cannot quarrel now for the possession of a woman. . . . She chose: remember that! . . . It was twenty-six years this September. We have lived our lives, you and I; we have lived out our lives, the good and the evil. Why should we now for the second time add passion to sorrow?"

"And yet knowing all you took me in!"

"Yes!" the old man cried almost proudly. "And I have made you again what you once were. . . . What *she* loved as you," he added to himself, "a man full of Power."

Then they were speechless in face of the fact: the one had taken all and the sweet love turned to acid in his heart, and the other had lost and the bitter turned to sweet! When a long time had passed the surgeon spoke timidly:

"It might have been so different for her with you! You loved her—more."

There was the light of a compassionate smile on the Master's lips as he replied:

"Yes, I loved her, too."

"And it changed things—for you!"

"It changed things. There might have been my St. Jerome's—my fame also. Instead, I came here with my boys. And here I shall die, please God."

The old Master then became silent, his face set in a dream of life, as it was, as it would have been; while the great surgeon of St. Jerome's thought such thoughts as had never passed before into his mind. The night wind had died at this late hour, and in its place there was a coldness of the turning season. The stars shone near the earth and all was silent with the peace of mysteries. The Master looked at the man beside him and said calmly:

"It is well as it is—all well!"

At last the surgeon rose and stood before the Master.

"I have learned the Secret," he said, "and now it is time for me to go."

He went up to the house through the little court and disappeared within the Inn, while the Master sat by the pool, his face graven like the face of an old man, who has seen the circle of life and understands. . . . The next morning there was much talk about Dr. Norton's disappearance, until some one explained that the surgeon had been suddenly called back to the city.

The news spread through the Brotherhood one winter that the old Inn had been burned to the ground, a bitter December night when all the water-taps were frozen. And the Master, who had grown deaf of late, had been caught in his remote chamber, and burned or rather suffocated. There were few men in the Inn at the time, it being the holiday season, and when they had fought their way to the old man's room, they found him lying on the lounge by the window, the lids fallen over the dark eyes and his face placid with sleep or contemplation. . . . They sought in vain for the reason of the fire— but why search for causes?

All those beautiful hills that we loved to watch as the evening haze gathered, the Master left in trust for the people of the State—many acres of waving forests. And the School continued in its old place, the Brothers looking after its wants and supplying it with means to continue its work. But the Inn was never rebuilt. The blackened ruins of buildings were removed and the garden in the court extended so that it covered the whole space where the Inn had stood. This was enclosed with a thick plantation of firs on all sides but that one which looked westward across the Intervale. The spot can be seen for miles around on the Albany hill side.

And when it was ready—all fragrant and radiant with flowers—they placed the Master there beside the pool, where he had loved to sit, surrounded by men. On the sunken slab his title was engraved—

THE MASTER OF THE INN